THE BRIDGE OF DREAMS

Lancaster Bridges Prequel

Sylvia Price

Penn and Ink Writing, LLC

Copyright © 2023 Sylvia Price

All rights reserved

This is a work of fiction. Names, characters, places, and incidents are either products of the author's imagination or are used fictitiously. Any similarity to actual events or locales or persons, living or dead, is entirely coincidental.

No part of this publication may be reproduced, stored in or introduced into a retrieval system, or transmitted, in any form, or by any means (electronic, mechanical, photocopying, recording, or otherwise) without the prior written permission of the copyright owner. The author acknowledges the trademarked status and trademark owners of various products referenced status and trademark owners of various products referenced in this work of fiction, which have been used without permission. The publication/use of the trademarks is not authorized, associated with or sponsored by the trademark owners.

CONTENTS

Title Page
Copyright
Stay Up to Date with Sylvia Price
Praise for Sylvia Price's Books
Other Books by Sylvia Price
Unofficial Glossary of Pennsylvania Dutch Words

Chapter One	1
Chapter Two	10
Chapter Three	15
Chapter Four	25
Chapter Five	30
Chapter Six	37
Chapter Seven	43
Chapter Eight	48
Chapter Nine	54
Chapter Ten	58
Books By This Author	67

About the Author 79

STAY UP TO DATE WITH SYLVIA PRICE

Subscribe to Sylvia's newsletter at newsletter.sylviaprice.com to get to know Sylvia and her family. It's also a great way to stay in the loop about new releases, freebies, promos, and more.

As a thank-you, you will receive several FREE exclusive short stories that aren't available for purchase.

HOPE
for Hannah's
LOVE
Amish Love Through the Seasons
SHORT STORY
SYLVIA PRICE

SYLVIA PRICE
EVE
AN ELIJAH COMPANION STORY

PRAISE FOR SYLVIA PRICE'S BOOKS

"Author Sylvia Price wrote a storyline that enthralled me. The characters are unique in their own way, which made it more interesting. I highly recommend reading this book. I'll be reading more of Author Sylvia Price's books."

"You can see the love of the main characters and the love that the author has for the main characters and her writing. This book is so wonderful. I cannot wait to read more from this beautiful writer."

"The storyline caught my attention from the very beginning and kept me interested throughout the entire book. I loved the chemistry between the characters."

"A wonderful, sweet and clean story with strong

characters. Now I just need to know what happens next!"

"First time reading this author, and I'm very impressed! I love feeling the godliness of this story."

"This was a wonderful story that reminded me of a glorious God we have."

"I encourage all to read this uplifting story of faith and friendship."

"I love Sylvia's books because they are filled with love and faith."

OTHER BOOKS BY SYLVIA PRICE

Sarah (The Amish of Morrissey County Prequel) – FREE
Sadie (The Amish of Morrissey County Book 1) – http://getbook.at/sadie
Bridget (The Amish of Morrissey County Book 2) – http://getbook.at/bridget
Abigail (The Amish of Morrissey County Book 3) – http://getbook.at/morrisseyabigail
Eliza (The Amish of Morrissey County Book 4) – http://getbook.at/eliza
Dorothy (An Amish of Morrissey County Christmas Romance) – http://getbook.at/dorothy
The Amish of Morrissey County Boxed Set – http://mybook.to/morrisseybox

❉ ❉ ❉

The Origins of Cardinal Hill (The Amish of Cardinal Hill Prequel) – FREE
The Beekeeper's Calendar (The Amish of Cardinal Hill Book 1) – http://getbook.at/beekeeperscalendar

The Soapmaker's Recipe (The Amish of Cardinal Hill Book 2) – http://getbook.at/soapmakersrecipe
The Herbalist's Remedy (The Amish of Cardinal Hill Book 3) – http://getbook.at/herbalistsremedy
The Amish of Cardinal Hill Complete Series – http://mybook.at/cardinalbox

❧ ❧ ❧

A Promised Tomorrow (The Yoder Family Saga Prequel) – FREE
Peace for Yesterday (The Yoder Family Saga Book 1) – http://getbook.at/peaceforyesterday
A Path for Tomorrow (The Yoder Family Saga Book 2) – http://getbook.at/pathfortomorrow
Faith for the Future (The Yoder Family Saga Book 3) – http://getbook.at/faithforthefuture
Patience for the Present (The Yoder Family Saga Book 4) – http://getbook.at/patienceforthepresent
Return to Yesterday (The Yoder Family Saga Book 5) – http://getbook.at/returntoyesterday
The Yoder Family Saga Boxed – http://getbook.at/yoderbox

❧ ❧ ❧

The Christmas Cards: An Amish Holiday Romance – http://getbook.at/christmascards

❧ ❧ ❧

The Christmas Arrival: An Amish Holiday Romance – http://getbook.at/christmasarrival

❋ ❋ ❋

Seeds of Spring Love (Amish Love Through the Seasons Book 1) – http://getbook.at/seedsofspring
Sprouts of Summer Love (Amish Love Through the Seasons Book 2) – http://getbook.at/sproutsofsummer
Fruits of Fall Love (Amish Love Through the Seasons Book 3) – http://getbook.at/fruitsoffall
Waiting for Winter Love (Amish Love Through the Seasons Book 4) – http://getbook.at/waitingforwinter
Amish Love Through the Seasons Boxed Set – http://getbook.at/amishseasons

❋ ❋ ❋

Jonah's Redemption: Book 1 – FREE
Jonah's Redemption: Book 2 – http://getbook.at/jonah2
Jonah's Redemption: Book 3 – http://getbook.at/jonah3
Jonah's Redemption: Book 4 – http://getbook.at/jonah4
Jonah's Redemption: Book 5 – http://getbook.at/jonah5
Jonah's Redemption Boxed Set – http://

getbook.at/jonahset

❦ ❦ ❦

Elijah: An Amish Story of Crime and Romance – http://getbook.at/elijah

❦ ❦ ❦

Songbird Cottage Beginnings (Pleasant Bay Prequel) – FREE
The Songbird Cottage (Pleasant Bay Book 1) – http://getbook.at/songbirdcottage
Return to Songbird Cottage (Pleasant Bay Book 2) – http://getbook.at/returntosongbird
Escape to Songbird Cottage (Pleasant Bay Book 3) – http://getbook.at/escapetosongbird
Secrets of Songbird Cottage (Pleasant Bay Book 4) – http://getbook.at/secretsofsongbird
Seasons at Songbird Cottage (Pleasant Bay Book 5) – http://getbook.at/seasonsatsongbird
The Songbird Cottage Boxed Set – http://getbook.at/songbirdbox

❦ ❦ ❦

The Crystal Crescent Inn (Sambro Lighthouse Book 1) – http://getbook.at/cci1
The Crystal Crescent Inn (Sambro Lighthouse Book 2) – http://getbook.at/cci2

The Crystal Crescent Inn (Sambro Lighthouse Book 3) – http://getbook.at/cci3
The Crystal Crescent Inn (Sambro Lighthouse Book 4) – http://getbook.at/cci4
The Crystal Crescent Inn (Sambro Lighthouse Book 5) – http://getbook.at/cci5
The Crystal Crescent Inn Boxed Set – http://getbook.at/ccibox

UNOFFICIAL GLOSSARY OF PENNSYLVANIA DUTCH WORDS

Ach – Oh

Amisch – Amish

Daed – dad

Danki – thanks

Dochder – daughter

Eldre – parents

Englisch/Englischer – non-Amish person

Familye – family

Gmay – local Amish community

Gott – God

Gude mariye – Good morning

Gude naamidaag – Good afternoon

Gut – good

Kumm – come

Maem – mom
Mann – husband/man
Nee – no
Rumspringa – running around period for Amish youth
Schweschder – sister
Ya – yes

CHAPTER ONE

"**Y**ou want to do what?!"

"Shh!" Hannah Fisher cautioned her younger sister in a loud whisper, looking furtively over her shoulder in the direction where their father was mucking out stalls on the opposite side of the barn.

Ruth's expression turned apologetic as she, too, glanced behind them to check that her blaring exclamation had not been overheard.

The systematic sound of a pitchfork banging against the side of the wheelbarrow continued sans interruption, and Hannah breathed an audible sigh of relief. She was not yet ready to manage the certain pushback from her father when he learned of her desire to attend classes at the local community college in Lancaster County and spread her wings to explore the outside world. Though she would have to tell her parents eventually—if she summoned the courage to go through with it—she was in no hurry to cause strife in her close-knit family. Especially since she wasn't even certain that her dreams would ever come to anything anyway.

Ruth's gaze shifted back to Hannah. "You know that *Daed* will never allow it," she whispered, careful to keep her voice low this time.

Hannah gave no reply as she resumed the rhythmic motion of milking one of the cows. She feared that her sister was correct. Yet, that didn't stop her thirsting for something more than the traditional life that was planned out for and expected of her.

"We'd better hurry up and finish here so we can return to the house and help *Maem* prepare breakfast," Hannah prodded her sister, who continued to sit motionless on the milking stool next to her.

Ruth complied, returning to her task without complaint and filling the milk pail in front of her. The younger girl seemed content to walk the path of previous generations, to live on a farm and learn what was required of her in becoming a good farmer's wife one day. If she had ever considered the possibility of choosing another path for herself, she never gave any indication of it. Hannah couldn't help but wonder if she was the only one who had these stirrings for something more.

Of course, Ruth was two years younger than Hannah. Perhaps she simply had not yet developed the self-assurance to question whether she wanted anything other than the familiar—or the courage necessary to contemplate stepping away from the well-trodden path and forging her own way. Even at twenty, Hannah wasn't sure that she was courageous enough to go against her parents' expectations for her. Despite the fact that her dreams compelled her to go in a completely different direction.

Although she wasn't ready to make that final decision yet, she feared that the time would soon come when she'd have to make a choice. And she was not at all certain of what she would choose.

Finished with the milking, Ruth followed Hannah's lead to stow away their stools. They worked in a comfortable silence as they led the cows back to their clean stalls.

"I'll feed the chickens," Ruth offered, securing the latch on the wooden enclosure. "You go on ahead."

With an appreciative nod, Hannah picked up the pails of fresh milk to carry them back to the farmhouse, while Ruth filled a bucket with feed for the chickens.

As she reached the door of the barn, a nicker from the horse that was used to pull the family's buggies and pony cart and help with the plowing and harvesting of the crops echoed within, followed by the voice of Jeremiah Fisher, her father, in response, murmuring in low tones.

The sun, already beginning to peek over the horizon in the east, painted the sky in a wash of brilliant yellow and orange as Hannah stepped into the dawning day. It was the start of a beautiful summer day filled with endless possibilities. Hopefully, the one that seemed to call to her the strongest wouldn't cause an enormous and potentially irreparable rift in her family.

Loud clucking bounced through the barnyard like popcorn as Ruth opened the door of the chicken coop and scattered the feed on the ground.

Breathing in the crisp fresh morning air, Hannah attempted to let go of her worries and concerns as she crossed the grass-covered yard leading to the farmhouse back door.

"Where's your *schweschder*?" her mother, Clara, asked as Hannah entered the kitchen after wiping her boots on the doormat.

"Ruth's feeding the chickens. She'll be in in just a minute."

Putting away the milk, Hannah moved alongside the older woman to help start cooking a hearty meal of eggs, sausage, and a hash of potatoes, onions, and peppers. All the ingredients had come from their family farm, from either the animals or the garden.

The back door banged shut behind Ruth, announcing her arrival, and the three women worked together in practiced synchrony to finish preparing the food and setting the table, which was situated mid-kitchen.

Hannah's father returned to the farmhouse after completing his morning chores a short time later, and the family sat down to the delicious breakfast.

The meal passed with the normal talk of everyone's plans for the day, focused mainly on what tasks and duties needed to be accomplished. There was nothing to indicate the day would be different from any other day that had come before. At least, not until all the food had been consumed and Hannah stood up to take her dirty plate to the sink.

"I'd like to speak with you, *Dochder*," her father said. "Leave the dishes for your *maem* and Ruth and *kumm* into the front room with me."

Hannah's stomach suddenly twisted like a wrung-out cloth. Had her father overheard her conversation with Ruth in the barn after all?

But no, his expression would surely not be so calm if he had. She briefly searched her sister's gaze and tried to draw comfort and courage from Ruth's reassuring smile. Hannah's nervousness, however, failed to abate; she could only think of one other matter her father might want to raise and discuss with her. And she was looking forward to it with even less enthusiasm than her proposed deviation from her Amish roots.

She sat down on the sofa in the living room while he settled into his normal seat in the wingback chair angled in front of the cold hearth. Gripping her hands tightly together in her lap, she waited for him to speak.

"Hannah, you've reached an age when it's time that you start thinking about marrying and having a *familye* of your own."

Of course she wanted those things one day. But there were other things that she hoped to do first—*needed* to do first—or she wouldn't be able to do them at all. Her dream of attending college would never happen once she married and started having children. Many of the young women among her peers were already wives—and some were even mothers or soon to be—but Hannah wasn't ready to settle down to that kind of life herself yet.

Her parents expected both Hannah and Ruth to marry and settle into a life of homemaking and raising a family, but as the eldest, it was Hannah who was expected to lead by example and follow tradition in doing so first.

"Samuel Stoltzfus has spoken to me about courting you, and I've given him my permission," her father continued, oblivious to the inner turmoil of her thoughts. "He's a *gut Amisch* man who will make a fine *mann*."

Her father's announcement did not completely rip the rug out from under Hannah's feet. Samuel Stoltzfus and his brother, Levi, lived on a neighboring farm, and they had been friends with Hannah and Ruth since the four of them were all young children. After the church service the past Sunday, Samuel had revealed his interest to be more than just friends with Hannah and indicated his intention to speak with her father.

She liked Samuel well enough, though not in that way. At least, not yet. And maybe not ever? But she hadn't been able to come up with an acceptable reason to refuse his attentions. After her father's declaration, however, the proverbial pulled rug shifted her off balance, and not only was she feeling anxious at the speed that things seemed to be moving along without her, but she also didn't have a clue what to do about it all.

Could love grow and blossom from the friendship she shared with Samuel?

But before she could consider whether or not she wanted to *marry* him, she first needed to decide if she was ready to get married *at all* right then. Or should she rather take the opportunity to pursue her dream for knowledge and experiences outside the Amish community?

As she tried to imagine herself living the two vastly different lives, she wondered which one would bring contentment.

Or would she eventually come to have regrets no matter which path she chose?

Ach, *how can I make a decision about my future when my mind is filled with so much confusion?*

Time was running out for Hannah. She could pacify her father for a little while by agreeing to go along with the courtship, but that would only work for so long before a marriage proposal would force her to decide what kind of life she truly wanted to live.

CHAPTER TWO

Later that day, Hannah decided to take a walk in the fields, hoping that the beauty of God's creation would help soothe her enough to make sense of her thoughts and bring some semblance of order to her tangled feelings.

Could she really put her own desire for independence ahead of the expectations of her parents and their community? Could she really go against their wishes?

Like a terrified fieldmouse when it realizes it has fallen within the piercing gaze of an owl, Hannah almost scurried for cover when she noticed Samuel working on the other side of the fence bordering her father's land. She wasn't sure that she wanted to talk to him right then. But she couldn't very well ignore him, especially since there was no doubt he had seen her, evidenced by his wave.

She turned toward him.

Is this the path that you want for me, Gott? she silently prayed. Was running into Samuel a sign?

She couldn't quite bring herself to see him as her husband, though. Could she ever come to love him as more than a friend?

"*Gude naamidaag,*" he called out as she neared the property line.

She reciprocated his greeting.

He dusted off his hands and drew closer, leaning against the fence separating them. "I'm glad to see you. I wanted to ask if you'd go driving with me on Sunday after church."

Hannah hesitated for a moment before accepting his invitation. "*Ya.*"

Samuel seemed to discern her lack of enthusiasm. Or perhaps she had not done a very good job of hiding it.

His dark eyebrows crinkled in concern. "What's the matter, Hannah? You haven't been yourself lately."

Should she tell him about her conflicted thoughts? Was it fair to burden him with her uncertainty? Or maybe it would be unfair to *not* share her doubts with him. Despite the fact that he hoped for a different depth of relationship between them, he was still her friend, and it didn't feel right to let him think that she was happy to go along with all of this when she plainly wasn't. At least, not right then.

How would he react if he knew the truth? Would he want to end the courtship before it had really begun? Or might he understand her desire to make her own choices and experience a different way of life before becoming a wife and mother took that option away from her?

She decided to reveal part of it to him and see how he received it. "I've been considering taking some classes at the community college fifteen miles away. I used one of the computers at the library to do a bit of research and learned that I'll need to pass a GED test before I can enroll." She subconsciously held her breath as she waited for Samuel's response.

Surprise blanketed his features. "It seems you've given this more than just a passing thought. And you're set on this course? This is what you want?"

"I'm not sure." And that was the truth. She wasn't completely certain whether she actually wanted to do it. But the one thing she *did* know was that she wasn't ready to close the door to the possibility of it.

Samuel's gaze bounced away from her, out across his land, and back to her. He inhaled deeply.

"Well, I can't tell you what to do. But I won't stand in your way if you decide that's what you want. We can still start courting…"

She nodded her agreement, feeling calmer about entering a courtship with Samuel now that she'd confessed the reason for her initial hesitation and he'd unexpectedly offered his support of her desire to assert her independence.

But after they parted ways, doubts rushed back in to plague her, like circling vultures zoning in on a carcass the second the predator lumbers away.

Even if Samuel hadn't opposed the notion of her attending college, she knew that her parents' reaction—disapproval—would not be so calm and collected. Not only would they be against her learning ways that were different from their beliefs, but it would include Hannah moving out from under their influence.

She didn't know if she could even pass the test necessary to be accepted for admittance into college. But she felt compelled to try. Her resolve solidified to secretly study for the GED exam during her next visit to the library.

That didn't mean her decision was final, however. This was only the first step in that direction, and she could change her mind at any point in time. Just because she started on this path, didn't mean she had to follow through to the end. Nothing prevented her from changing trajectory and making a different choice later.

She loved her family and community. She wanted neither to be at odds with her parents nor to completely abandon their beliefs, but there was no denying that her heart yearned for something more than just the life they envisioned for her.

What was the right thing to do?

CHAPTER THREE

Samuel finished his work for the day and headed toward the farmhouse he shared with Levi, all the while mulling over Hannah Fisher's unexpected revelation. Before that day, he'd had no idea that she wanted anything other than to be a wife and mother—as was expected of the women in their community.

Despite his own inclination to a traditional Amish life, he found his affection for Hannah opening him up to the idea of being supportive in her desire to study new things. Although he did have some reservations about her living in the *Englisch* world to attend college in furthering her education, he had not discouraged her from contemplating it.

As long as she was questioning what she truly wanted and looking to things outside of their community, it would not be wise to marry. If he'd forced her to make a choice then, she might've still agreed to be courted by him, but it would be shortsighted to think that it wouldn't cause her to grow to resent him later, casting doubt and uncertainty on their happiness in the years ahead.

If they were truly meant to be together as man and wife, he had to believe that God would lead her back to him after she had a chance to explore the outside world and all it offered.

It was imperative that Hannah make her own choice without any influence from Samuel trying to sway her in any direction; his role was to be supportive of her. That was the only way she would truly find contentment in being a wife and mother one day.

It wasn't overwhelmingly daunting for Samuel because he trusted that the Lord was guiding them and this was part of His plan. A part of him, though, was still hesitant about the unchartered journey ahead even though he felt confident of the destination.

As Samuel entered the house, his brother greeted him.

"I saw you talking to Hannah earlier. Are you two officially courting now?" Levi asked.

"*Ya.*"

"Then why don't you look happier about it?"

Perhaps talking over things with Levi would help Samuel sort out his mixed feelings of faith and trepidation. With that hope in mind, he relayed what Hannah had told him.

Levi's mouth twisted in censure. "You're a fool to allow this. You should put a stop to it right now before it goes anywhere."

Samuel realized he should probably have expected Levi to voice his objection so strongly. Although a small but growing faction of people in town supported a more progressive way of life—and would surely stand behind Hannah seeking a higher education—Levi had never made any secret of the fact that he was not among their number. Instead, his brother and others like him were very vocal in their stance against any kind of deviation from tradition. Their sole aim was to preserve the conservative Old Order Amish ways, to keep it uncorrupted and untainted by the *Englisch* world.

While Samuel leaned towards favoring a traditional Amish life for himself, he had come to realize that people could differ in their opinions on such matters but still truly love God and live lives that honored Him. Unfortunately, this resulted in him feeling increasingly caught in the middle of the two opposing groups.

"Well, Hannah might decide against attending college," he said, hoping to forestall an argument with his brother over their differing positions on the matter.

Levi volleyed back with a sneer, "Or she might decide to go and live in the *Englisch* world and fill her head with a bunch of rubbish ideas that oppose our beliefs. I can't believe you're actually encouraging her in this by not outright forbidding it. Don't tell me that you're turning into one of those who are pushing to change things and corrupt our *Amisch* ways?"

"*Nee*," Samuel replied gently, purposefully keeping his tone moderate and respectful.

"*Gut*. See that it stays that way. If *you* won't put a stop to Hannah's foolishness, maybe *I* will."

"What do you mean?" asked Samuel, struggling to maintain his temperate composure.

Levi folded his arms across his chest, his expression hardening. "I think I should go and have a talk with her *daed*."

"This is none of your concern, Levi," Samuel protested. "Please, stay out of it."

Levi's mien clearly showed he didn't agree, but fortunately he dropped the subject.

Samuel prayed that would be the end to it. Still,

he wondered if he should warn Hannah that his brother might reveal her secret.

Or was Levi simply making an empty threat? Surely, he wouldn't involve himself in something that was no concern of his.

* * *

The lantern on the nightstand cast light on the pages of the Bible open in her lap as Hannah sat on her bed. But try as she might, she could not concentrate on the passages in front of her. Her jumbled thoughts were filled with all that had transpired that day.

She had been pleasantly surprised by Samuel's understanding that afternoon and that he didn't try to discourage her from attending college. Honestly, she wouldn't have been shocked if he'd voiced some opposition since she knew he wanted a traditional life himself—and must have expected that she would play the role of a traditional wife when he was first considering courting her. But he hadn't turned his back on her after she revealed something that had the potential to unsettle his plans. Instead, he encouraged her to choose her own path.

Perhaps that should have made the decision

easier for her; unfortunately, it didn't.

It was regrettable indeed that her father would not be so open-minded about her secret desire.

The older man had been over the moon that evening when Hannah told her family at supper that Samuel invited her to go driving that Sunday after church. In her father's mind, her future was already set.

"Hannah, can I talk to you about something?"

Hannah looked up at her younger sister standing in the open doorway of her bedroom. "Of course, Ruth," she replied, closing her Bible and setting it aside.

Ruth stepped into the room and shut the door behind her, then hesitated.

"What's on your mind?" Hannah coaxed.

Despite her encouraging tone, it was several seconds before Ruth elaborated further. "I've been thinking about what you told me in the barn this morning. So it came as a surprise when you announced that you and Samuel have started courting. I guess that means you've decided not to attend classes at college after all."

"*Nee.*" Hannah corrected her sister's misconception.

Ruth's eyebrows knit together in confusion. "I

don't understand. If you're planning to marry…"

"No one's talking about marriage yet," Hannah amended. *Well, except for* Daed, she silently added. But since marriage was a matter to be decided between Hannah and Samuel—not her parents—she didn't see any point in mentioning that detail in that moment. "I actually spoke to Samuel today about wanting to go to college," she continued. "And he was not averse to the possibility."

"Really?" Surprise suffused Ruth's face.

Hannah nodded, and Ruth's expression shifted.

"I'm glad you haven't given in to the pressure of conforming and changed your mind." Ruth fell silent but didn't make a move to leave the room.

"Is there something…else on your mind?" Hannah prompted.

Ruth moved away from the door, pleating the fabric of her dark blue skirt between her fingers. "Well, learning that you want something different than what is expected of us, too—"

"Too?" Hannah interrupted, needing to make sure she was not misunderstanding her sister's meaning. "*You* also want something different?"

❉ ❉ ❉

Ruth bit her lip before admitting the truth. "Our conversation this morning got me thinking about how *Daed* has always discouraged my interest in art. It might seem like a silly dream compared to yours, but I've always wanted to pursue it. And not just as a hobby I dabble in here and there."

Ruth delighted in drawing scenes from nature and local landmarks and buildings. Her father had always made it plain that he considered it a waste of time, though. But Ruth, after her recent wonderings, contemplated whether it would be possible to support herself with her talent if she studied and learned different techniques.

The Amish handicraft store in town sold locally made quilts, knitting, and wood carvings. Maybe Ruth could convince the owner to display her work, too. That was assuming he would not be against the idea because he thought her art served no practical purpose.

Might people actually want to buy her drawings someday? Or was that just unrealistic wishful thinking?

"I don't think that's a silly dream at all, Ruth," Hannah's voice broke into her thoughts.

The corners of Ruth's mouth curved up in a small smile at her sister's words. "*Danki*. I just meant that I understand having a desire for something more, something that is not considered the norm by the Old Order simply because of tradition and not because the Bible forbids or opposes it—and feeling torn between following your own dreams and meeting the expectations of our *eldre*."

"I had no idea you felt this way," Hannah admitted.

"I didn't know you felt this way, either. Not until you said something earlier today. I think you should do it. Go to college, I mean," she clarified, wanting at least one of them to be able to fulfill their dreams.

"But making the decision is not so simple. There are a lot of factors to consider." Hannah's shoulders shagged. "What about *Daed*? He'll no doubt be angry, and it will cause a huge fight."

But Ruth suspected that was not the only reason Hannah wanted to avoid a confrontation—and her next words confirmed it.

"I don't want to disappoint him."

Ruth sank down on to the bed beside her sister and sighed. "Neither do I. It's all well and good to dream about forging a different path, but it's a lot harder to actually do it, isn't it?"

"*Ya*." Hannah reached over and squeezed Ruth's hand.

"Maybe if we support each other..." Ruth started, then trailed off, not sure that it would do any good.

Would the knowledge that she had Hannah on her side suffice in giving Ruth the courage she needed to forge ahead in the face of her parents' certain disapproval of her actions? She could only hope so.

Hannah didn't appear to share her silent doubts. "While I'm in town tomorrow running errands, I intend to visit the library and start reading some books to help me study for the test I need to take before I can apply to college. Why don't you *kumm* with me and spend some time working on your drawings?" she suggested.

"All right," Ruth agreed, despite her lingering misgivings.

CHAPTER FOUR

With each step on her walk home from the library the next day, Hannah prayed to God for guidance. She abhorred keeping secrets from her father. Just imagining how he would react if she admitted to what she had been doing in addition to her errands spurred her on in prayer. Was it possible that he might surprise her, though?

However, Hannah didn't get a chance to confess before her father confronted her on the issue. He already knew about her desire to attend college. But how? Ruth, for sure, would not have broken her confidence. She wouldn't have had the opportunity to do so anyway since she had been in town with Hannah.

Her father soon revealed the source of the information: Levi. The only way that he could've known was if Samuel had told him, but she didn't blame her friend for confiding in his brother. She had thought that Levi was her friend, too, but she wasn't so sure after her father's disclosure. Levi had recently joined a group in town that shared his views and was determined to maintain the old ways, actively opposing any sort of change or outside influence in their community.

"You want to turn your back on our beliefs and abandon the *Amisch* ways?" her father asked angrily.

"*Nee, Daed.* I was just thinking of taking a delayed *Rumspringa* to attend classes." Until she was married and baptized in the church, the opportunity to gain knowledge and experiences outside the community amongst the *Englisch* was permissible without judgement or condemnation.

That silenced her father. Although he clearly did not approve of this choice, he could hardly not follow the accepted custom of allowing her this bit of freedom to do as she wished without censure. However, she did not fool herself into thinking that meant he wouldn't try to change her mind.

She still wasn't sure that her mind was made up yet, though. She continued to be buffeted on the Sea of Indecision by the relentless waves of opposing voices in her head.

"You must do what you feel *Gott* is calling you

to," her father stated, breaking into her thoughts.

Was this what God wanted for her? Or had she blinded herself to the Lord's will because she was so focused on her own wishes?

Was it really possible to preserve her commitment to her faith while still pursuing her curiosity at experiencing life outside the community?

Things were tense enough between the conservative and progressive factions in town already. Would this only exacerbate the situation, adding fuel to the flames? She didn't want to bear that responsibility.

She shared her worries with Samuel during their drive that Sunday.

"Maybe if I tried to talk to Levi—" she started but stopped short when Samuel shook his head before she could even finish.

"It won't do any good," he objected despondently. "Unless you've decided not to attend college."

"*Nee.*" She hadn't decided that. But…

This wasn't just causing strife within her own family; it could potentially widen the rift in the community, too.

Was pursuing her aspirations really worth the

risk?

* * *

Levi hadn't raised the subject of Hannah again in Samuel's presence, but it was clear Levi wasn't being silent about it to others. His censure of Samuel's refusal to make her conform to a traditional role was putting unwanted pressure on Samuel to choose a side. But perhaps he already had —by supporting Hannah's right to make her own choices.

"I'm sorry I provided Levi with the ammunition to go to your *daed* and reveal your secret," he apologized.

Hannah sighed from her seat in the buggy beside him. "It's not your fault. But I'm so confused and don't know what I should do."

Samuel held his silence, determined not to give her advice or try to steer her in any particular direction. Though this was certainly not how he had envisioned starting a life with Hannah, he didn't know whether he wanted her to reconsider attending college or not.

He secretly suspected that she would soon get over this hurdle and carry on with her plans despite her professed hesitations. But he wasn't sure how he felt about the fact that she wanted to leave their community while he stayed behind and continued working his farm.

Although he tried to convince himself that she would return eventually after her *Rumspringa* and be happy to become his wife and mother of his children, he couldn't disregard the possibility that she might ultimately decide to leave the Amish faith after she had a chance to experience life in the *Englisch* world.

But he kept his doubts to himself; Hannah didn't need further confusion with a reason to end their courtship before it even started. And even though he was uncertain whether it would ever actually lead to marriage, he was not yet ready to give up all hope that things could work out between them. Somehow.

CHAPTER FIVE

When Ruth proposed another session at the library the following week, Hannah declined. Ruth, appreciating that her sister's recent unpleasant exchange with their father was the catalyst for Hannah's second thoughts, nevertheless tried her utmost to change Hannah's mind, but she stoically refused to be swayed.

"Maybe I should stay at home too, then," Ruth suggested though it was not what she wanted to do at all.

"*Nee*, go on without me," Hannah insisted.

It didn't take much to persuade Ruth, who subsequently hitched the horse to the pony cart and headed into town. As the horse clip-clopped past the town's central park, her gaze was drawn to an *Englisch* woman with an easel set up under the shade of a tree, using a broad brush to make sweeping strokes across the canvas. Her curiosity instantly piqued, Ruth, almost without conscious thought, stopped the pony cart and clambered down to investigate what the artist was painting. Ruth's sound of appreciation caught the other woman's attention, and she turned to glance at Ruth.

"I didn't mean to interrupt you," Ruth said with an apologetic smile.

"I like when people show an interest in my work. That's why I decided to paint here instead of at my apartment." She set down her brush, wiped her paint-stained fingers on a rag, and extended her hand toward Ruth. "I'm Adeline."

Ruth accepted the handshake and introduced herself. "Are you just visiting the area?" she asked.

"No. I moved here a few weeks ago, but I'm hoping to sell some of my paintings and eventually rent a studio and open an art gallery in town."

"I'm an artist, too." The statement slipped unbidden from Ruth's mouth without conscious prompting from her brain, and she immediately felt the need to backpedal. "Or I should say, I hope to be one someday."

Adeline was not dissuaded by her demur, however. "I'd love to take a look at your work if you'd be willing to show it to me."

Ruth hesitated momentarily. But after seeing Adeline's painting—even though it was only half finished—she really wanted to know what such a talented artist thought of her own drawings.

She excused herself to retrieve her bag from the pony cart and then returned, clutching her sketchbook to her chest. She paused for another long moment before she finally handed over the pad of drawing paper.

"Please give me your honest opinion," she said, then waited nervously for Adeline's verdict as the woman flipped slowly through the pages.

"Your drawings are *really* good," Adeline pronounced.

"You truly think so?"

"Yes, I do. You have a natural ability, a gift."

Ruth blushed at the uncommon adulation. "*Danki*. I mean, thank you," she corrected herself.

"Have you considered trying painting? You could create some beautiful landscapes using acrylic paints," Adeline suggested.

"I've never tried my hand at it. But if you think I should…"

"I do," Adeline replied firmly.

Ruth nodded in mute assent. "Well, I'll let you get back to your painting now."

Adeline picked up her paintbrush. "I enjoyed meeting you, Ruth. I hope I'll see you again soon."

"Me, too."

Ruth encountered Adeline painting in the park several more times over the next week, and a friendship quickly developed between them. She wanted to share her exciting news with her sister, but she held back because she knew that Hannah's thoughts were consumed with other concerns.

❋ ❋ ❋

The resistance from her father had caused Hannah to reconsider the wisdom of pursuing additional education at college when her parents and many in the community were so ardently against it. But she finally concluded that she wasn't willing to allow the voices of dissent to dictate her actions. Not when there were people who had shown their support in various ways, like Samuel and Ruth.

When Hannah announced that she wanted to accompany Ruth to town to resume studying at the library for the GED test, her sister responded with enthusiasm and a wide smile stretched across her face.

They worked together to hitch up the pony cart,

then set out toward town together.

Ruth fidgeted on the seat beside Hannah. "I'm glad you decided to *kumm* with me today. There's someone I'd like you to meet."

"Who?"

"A new friend. Her name is Adeline McCarthy."

Ruth told Hannah all about meeting the *Englisch* artist. But despite her own desire to explore the outside world, Hannah didn't know how she felt about a non-Amish person coming in to their community when tensions between the progressive and conservative members were already so high.

Should she encourage Ruth's friendship with the other woman? Or was it hypocritical for Hannah to consider curtailing with whom her sister interacted when she herself would be surrounded by an entire campus of non-Amish people should she end up attending college?

Perhaps I should reserve judgment for now. At least until after I've actually met Adeline. That would help her to make up her own mind about whether the newcomer in town might prove to unwittingly stir the trouble pot.

They reached the park in which Ruth had explained Adeline liked to paint. Her easel was already set up, and she was busy at work.

Ruth performed introductions between Adeline and Hannah. "Adeline has been teaching me about new techniques and using different media," she added, her animated expression conveying the excitement she experienced talking about her art.

"Your sister is very talented," Adeline informed Hannah.

"Not nearly as talented as you," Ruth protested though her cheeks turned pink with pleasure. "What are you working on now?" she asked, ensuring the conversation stayed focused on Adeline rather than herself.

Adeline stepped back to afford them a full view of the canvas. "I'm just putting the finishing touches on this scene of children on the playground."

The bright reds and vibrant yellows in which the little ones were dressed contrasted with the muted gray and black of the swings and slides. Adeline had so perfectly captured their expressions of innocent joy and wonder as they laughed and played together.

Hannah was impressed with how Adeline's use of light and shadows made the picture come alive; one felt as though they were standing in the midst of the scene. In fact, the painting could easily be mistaken for a photograph at first glance.

Even though the Amish didn't condone depictions of human images, whether sketches, portraits, or photos—or the creation of art for its own sake—Hannah could appreciate the beauty in Adeline's painting of *Englisch* children.

As they talked a bit more, Hannah discovered that she quite liked the *Englisch* woman and was inspired by her passion for her work. But she was also apprehensive that conservative members like Levi would contest having this outside influence in their Amish community—and that Adeline's presence would cause more conflict between the opposing factions.

The situation had worsened over recent weeks, and she feared even the littlest thing could light a match to the volatile situation. Would this be what broke their fractured community?

Despite this trepidation, Hannah and Ruth continued to meet up with Adeline whenever they went to town and found her painting in the park.

Hannah, too, quickly came to have affection for Adeline, a dear friend who supported her dream to attend college and Ruth's longing to enrich her art.

CHAPTER SIX

Ruth and Hannah arrived at the park one afternoon only to stumble upon Levi and several other Amish men openly condemning Adeline, their raised angry voices edged with hostility.

"You don't belong here," Levi enunciated through gritted teeth, his features twisted in a nasty sneer. "You should leave and go back to wherever you came from."

Ruth hurried toward her friend, Hannah close on her heels.

"What's going on?" Hannah asked in bewilderment, inserting herself between Adeline and Levi.

Her interference, however, did nothing to calm the fiery situation.

Levi ignored Hannah as though she were invisible. "Your outside influence is corrupting our community," he continued menacingly. "And you can be sure I intend to put an end to it." With his threat lingering heavily in the air, he turned on his heel and left, the other men following behind him.

"What was that all about?" Hannah asked, her eyebrows raised in shock and concern.

Adeline wrung her hands. "I've started a new series of paintings, and I'm afraid those men took offense at the subject matter." Though she tried to downplay the incident, it was clear that it had left her shaken.

Ruth noticed the smears of paint obscuring whatever scene Adeline had been creating on her canvas. "They ruined your painting?" she asked in disbelief.

"Oh, no," Adeline explained. "They startled me when they appeared out of the blue just as I had opened a tube of paint to add more to my palette. I inadvertently squirted it all over the canvas and then made this dreadful mess when I tried to wipe it up."

Was that really the truth? It sounded plausible enough. But Ruth knew that Levi hadn't hesitated for even a second before causing trouble between Hannah and their father by exposing her secret desire to attend classes at college.

She tried to press Adeline for more details of what exactly had transpired before she and Hannah arrived.

The other woman declined any further talk on the matter, her face flushed a deep hot red.

Just how far would Levi and his accomplices go in their bid to preserve the old traditions?

Ruth wouldn't put much past him; after all, he was resolved to go to any length to keep outside influences from bringing unwanted changes to their community.

❈ ❈ ❈

When Samuel first learned of the controversy surrounding Adeline's art, he had tried to stay well out of it. With the community already fractured, this new issue was the last thing they needed. Too many others had already taken sides, with neighbor against neighbor and former friends turning into adversaries. Even families were being split apart by their opposing views.

The community had become increasingly divided over the uproar caused by the *Englischer's* new paintings. Many of the more progressive members, including Hannah and Ruth, supported her right to create her artwork and live here without interference, while an equal number of others had joined Levi and his group in voicing their opinion that Adeline should be forced to leave the area.

Samuel sat in a chair at the back of the meeting that had been called to discuss the situation with Adeline and her art. He listened silently as arguments were volleyed back and forth as to what should be done.

"She's not one of us," Levi insisted, his expression hardening.

"Adeline isn't the only *Englischer* who lives around here," Hannah countered.

"True, but unlike the rest of them, she's blatantly flaunting her disregard for the *Amisch* church," an older man grumbled.

"That's right," Levi interjected. "Not only is she painting *Amisch* people, which is bad enough, but even worse than that, she's intending to sell those pictures to tourists."

There were several murmurs of agreement around the room.

The conservative members of the community wanted to uphold the church's traditional sanction against sketches and portraits of human images. It wasn't enough that Adeline stop painting scenes featuring the Amish; Levi and his ilk wanted her gone.

Samuel did not agree with that extreme stance, but this fraught situation made him evaluate just how much outside influence *should* be permitted, especially when it could so easily cause such offense—no matter how unintentional—and added to the existing tensions between the opposing factions in the local Amish community.

He stood up from his chair and cleared his throat. "I have no quarrel with people making their own decisions and living as they see fit. But when an *Englischer* shows up in our town and infringes on the beliefs of members of our *gmay* in a way that directly affects them, that's when I have to speak up."

He felt too strongly about the importance of tradition in this instance to continue holding his tongue in a bid to try to appease everyone.

❊ ❊ ❊

Hannah could understand Samuel's point of view that Amish tradition was important, based on valid principles, and intended to set the community apart from the *Englisch* world, but she still felt compelled to stand in solidarity with

Ruth, to defend their friend who'd never shown any prejudice against their Amish beliefs and didn't know at the time that she was doing something that would cause offense. Unfortunately, many believed that ignorance of their customs was not a good enough justification to excuse Adeline's transgression.

Hannah didn't like being on opposite sides of the fence as Samuel, though.

Once all the arguments had been heard, a vote was taken as to whether Adeline would be formally asked to leave the area. Hannah doubted such a verdict could be enforced, but fortunately the vote went in favor of allowing Adeline to stay. It was only by a very small margin, but at least the alternative wouldn't be put to the test. Many were unhappy with the decision—if the angry muttering she heard as she left the meeting was anything to go by.

Hannah slipped away without talking to Samuel, not knowing what to say to him after ending up on different sides of the debate which his side had just lost.

CHAPTER SEVEN

Samuel was grappling over whether he should continue in his courtship of Hannah after recent events had suddenly thrown his future into question. While he recognized and respected Hannah's right to make her own choices, her decision to defend Adeline had put her at complete odds with him.

Was a marriage between them unwise when they held such different views about what they wanted in their own lives? As children, they shared so much in common, but maybe they had since grown too far in opposite directions to be able to turn their friendship into something more.

He would never ask Hannah to set aside her dream for his sake. Not if that wasn't what she chose to do of her own volition. But did that mean he would have to give up on his own dream of having her as his wife?

His feelings for her had already deepened, but he didn't know if she reciprocated his feelings to the same depth. *Will she ever be able to love me as more than a friend?* he mused.

※ ※ ※

After the supper dishes were washed and put away, Hannah sat down at the kitchen table to study. Now that her desire to take college classes was out in the open, she'd started checking out books on preparing for the GED test from the library and bringing them home. Her father eyed the study guides with disapproval but didn't say anything.

Hannah worked diligently for several hours until she was stifling yawns and struggling to keep her eyes open. When the words on the page in front of her blurred, she finally closed the book and headed to bed. Hours later, she was awoken from a deep sleep by loud shouting. Tossing back the blanket, she jumped up to see what was going on. As she rushed to the window to pull back the curtains, she became aware that her bedroom was illuminated by an eerie orange glow. A loud gasp escaped her at the shocking sight: the entire barn was engulfed in flames!

Hannah raced from the room and made her way outside. She could hear the shrill whinnying of their horse and the panicked lowing of cows. She darted forward without any thought other than to save them.

Her father stepped into her path, blocking her attempts, and grabbed on to her when she tried to veer around him. "Stay back, Hannah," he cautioned.

"But the animals—"

"The fire's too far along. It's too dangerous to try to go inside to get them out."

Tears sprang to her eyes and streamed down her cheeks.

Ruth's arms snaked around her, and Hannah hugged her sister tight as they cried in grief for the terrible tragedy.

Their parents mirrored their silhouettes against the fire-illuminated night just a short distance away, with Jeremiah Fisher comforting his weeping wife. His own eyes remained dry, his expression stoic, though he was surely feeling just as devastated by the loss as the rest of his family.

The towering flames lit up the night with the heat so intense that it forced them all to stay well back as they helplessly witnessed the barn burning.

Sirens sounded in the distance and gradually

grew closer. *An* Englischer *in the area must have spotted the flames and called it in to the emergency services*, Hannah figured.

A few minutes later, the barnyard was abuzz with firemen shouting orders and maneuvering their equipment. The loud spray of water rushing from the pressurized hoses mixed with the noise of the raging fire.

The firefighters worked all night to put out the blaze. As the last of the embers surrendered to the spray, the sun was just starting to lighten the sky in the east.

Charred rubble was all that remained of the barn. The acrid smell of smoke blanketed the devastating site. Not only had they lost the building but all the livestock and equipment inside, too. Only the chickens were spared due to the fortuitous fact that their coop was situated far enough away that the flames and sparks hadn't reached it.

It wasn't until the next day that the wreckage was cool enough to go near, and the authorities arrived to pick through the remains to determine the cause of the fire. Hannah was standing outside with her father watching the activity when an *Englisch* man broke away from the others and approached them.

His expression was grim as he introduced himself as the Lancaster County fire investigator. "This was arson; the fire was started deliberately."

Hannah gasped in disbelief at this pronouncement.

"You're certain?" her father asked.

"Yes. There's no doubt in my mind. But I'll need to do some further investigation to establish who set the fire." He excused himself and returned to the crime scene.

Hannah stood frozen, her emotions a tangle of pain and confusion.

Who could have done this to our family? And why? How could it be possible that someone in the community hated them enough to justify such a malicious act?

Why had God allowed this to happen?

CHAPTER EIGHT

Samuel arrived at the Fishers' farm a few days later to join in with the communal cleanup efforts after the authorities finished collecting evidence for their investigation. Several other neighbors joined him. He made excuses for his brother's noticeable absence, explaining that Levi was attending a livestock auction in the next county. But the skepticism on many faces testified that they viewed the fact that his brother wasn't there as an admission of guilt.

It was not proof Levi had a hand in starting the fire, of course. However, Samuel was not oblivious to the rumblings that Levi and his group were responsible for the arson. No one said anything directly to Samuel, but he overheard more than a few whispers—both accusing Levi and in defense of him.

Samuel just kept his head down and continued

to work, not wanting to get drawn into a contentious debate with anyone. There was much speculation about whether the authorities would find evidence to bring the perpetrators to justice. But everyone already seemed to have formed their own opinions about what they believed happened. And the two groups were at odds about more than just whether Levi was innocent or guilty.

The individuals who counted themselves among the conservative faction were vocal about the fact that they thought *Englisch* authorities shouldn't be involved in what happened on an Amish-owned farm, while the more progressive contingent argued in favor of allowing whatever was necessary to find the culprits and punish them for their crime.

Even when they came together to help someone in need, heated arguments still broke out between conservative and progressive because of their fundamentally differing views. It was becoming increasingly clear that it might be impossible for the two groups to come to a consensus as to the direction they wanted for their community going into the future.

This was merely a temporary truce, and Samuel feared that hostilities would flare up again all too soon.

* * *

Hannah placed a tray of sandwiches on the table that had been set up outside as her mother called the men to lunch. She watched Samuel approaching, soot and grime from carrying heavy chunks of burned beams to a wagon to haul away covering his clothing, face, and hands.

She had spent the morning helping her mother make food and offering water to everyone who came to assist her family as they cleared away the debris from the fire. All the while, she'd found herself sneaking glances at Samuel as he worked.

There was no denying he was a good and caring man who would be a wonderful husband and father one day.

He removed his hat as he reached her, revealing a strip of soot-free skin across the top of his forehead. "Will you sit with me to eat after I get washed up?" he asked.

"*Ya*," she agreed.

A short time later, they were filling their plates with food and retrieving glasses of lemonade. They found a shady spot beneath a large oak tree near the boundary separating the Fishers' land from Samuel's. Once settled on the ground, they ate in silence for a few minutes.

Samuel sipped his lemonade, then cleared his throat. "How is your studying going?"

"*Gut*, I think," she said but didn't elaborate further.

"You usually tell me all about the interesting new things you've learned whenever we meet. So, what's wrong?"

She set down her half-eaten sandwich and sighed. "I'm worried about leaving my *familye* right now if I decide to go to college." For the first time, she had been forced to really think about the fact that in order to attend classes on a campus fifteen miles away, she would have to move away from home—and just what that really would mean.

"I'll be here to help them," Samuel assured her. "And they'll have the support of many others in the *gmay* as well. Just look at all the people who are here today."

"I know you're right. But…what about the fall harvest? It's in less than two months, and now we don't have a horse or plow or anything else we'll need to harvest the crops."

"I can supply all that," he again assured her.

"This setback shouldn't be the reason you give up on continuing your education."

His words inspired a sudden thought. Was stopping her from going to college the intention of whomever had started the fire? If so, how could she let them win by abandoning her dream?

But neither did she want to feel as though she was leaving her family in the lurch during such a difficult time.

Gott, I don't know what to do. Please, show me Your way, she prayed, feeling an instant sense of peace come over her at laying her troubles before the Lord.

Hannah knew that Samuel had meant his earlier words about continuing to lend her family a helping hand. She was grateful for how supportive he was of her dreams even after they had differed on how the situation with Adeline should be handled.

Finishing the last bit of his sandwich, Samuel dusted off his hands. "I guess I'd best get back to work now."

"I'll take your empty plate and glass back to the house for you," she offered.

"*Danki.*"

As she headed toward the kitchen with the dirty dishes, she glanced back over her shoulder at Samuel.

If she did decide to leave, it would not be forever. The possibility that she might decide not to come back was negligible. No matter what new things she experienced in the outside world, her family was here, and this was her home. In her heart, she knew it always would be.

But would Samuel be willing to be apart for so long? Would he grow tired of waiting for her to be ready to marry him?

CHAPTER NINE

As Ruth worked beside Hannah weeding the garden, she rocked back on her haunches and paused to glance up at the charred ground where the barn had stood just a few days before. She shivered despite the warmth of the sunny day.

Had this happened because of Hannah and Ruth's support of Adeline? That's what was being said around town—that the fire was set in retaliation for things not going the way Levi and his group had wanted at the community meeting.

The possibility filled Ruth with gnawing guilt that her entire family might be suffering because of her actions. Her parents had nothing to do with the controversy, yet they were the ones hurt most by the fire. Did people blame her mother and father for not putting a stop to the friendship between their daughters and an *Englischer*?

But if this all *was* because of Adeline, Ruth wondered why the *Englisch* woman had not been targeted personally. That would likely have actually succeeded in making her choose to leave the area, which surely must have been Levi's goal. Ruth didn't believe that he had simply given up on that just because he failed to gain the backing of the majority of the community. However, the fact that Adeline lived in town also increased the chances of being seen by witnesses.

No one had admitted to seeing anything the night the Fishers' barn was deliberately set aflame. There had been no word yet from the county authorities as to whether they'd found evidence pointing to a specific perpetrator. No one had been named an official suspect for the crime. Would the offenders continue to escape punishment?

Hannah's voice pulled Ruth from her musings. "I passed the GED test and applied at the community college. But I might not get in."

"You'll get in," Ruth replied with certainty. "But will you actually go?"

The fire had steered Ruth to reconsider continuing on her current path with her art, and she wondered if the same might be true for her sister with her studies, too. If their friendship and support of Adeline was really the reason this had happened, then how could Ruth seriously think of pursuing her own art at the risk of further hurt to her family?

She wanted to give art lessons to others to pass on the techniques that Adeline had taught her. But she knew that there'd be many who wouldn't approve of such an endeavor. Was following her own dreams worth causing more conflict between her neighbors and friends? Things already felt near breaking point, and she didn't want to be the match that made the powder keg finally explode and burned everything down.

Would Ruth have to leave the community to have any chance of realizing her dream? That was the choice that her elder sister was facing in that moment.

Hannah sank back on her heels between the rows of vegetables. "I don't know. I haven't decided anything yet. I still want to go and attend classes. But I need to pray about it to determine whether or not it's what *Gott* wants for me, too."

Perhaps Ruth should look to the Lord for guidance as well. Were her wishes really so selfish? Was wanting something for herself necessarily a bad thing?

What was the right choice given what had

already happened?

CHAPTER TEN

Samuel finished replacing the damaged fence board and straightened, wiping the back of his arm against his damp forehead. The morning sun beat down on him, and he adjusted his hat to shield his eyes from the glare. Setting down the hammer, he picked up his canteen of water and took a swig.

It had been almost two weeks since the Fishers' barn was destroyed, and the barren plot of scorched earth still scarred the landscape. Like many others in the community, Samuel couldn't help entertaining the suspicion that Levi and his friends played some part in setting the fire. But he couldn't bring himself to confront his brother about it.

Uncorroborated suspicions weren't enough to charge someone with wrongdoing, in any case. No physical substantiation had been found, so the county authorities could do nothing.

The crime remained unsolved despite the best efforts of the fire investigators. But God knew whose heart had been turned against Hannah's family. Whoever was responsible would not escape His judgment.

"*Gude mariye*, Samuel," Hannah called out, drawing his attention.

He glanced toward her, taking in the way the slight breeze teased strands of her hair that had escaped their confinement and accentuated the hint of pink in her cheeks.

She reached up to catch an errant lock and tucked it behind her ear. "I wanted to talk to you. Will you *kumm* for a walk with me?"

"Of course," he agreed, ducking through the split rail fence to join her.

They set off at a slow pace, but she didn't immediately speak.

"What did you *kumm* to talk to me about?" he finally prompted after several minutes of silence.

"I wanted to tell you that I've enrolled in a course at the community college and my classes start in a few weeks."

He stopped walking and placed his hands in his pockets. "So you're really going to do this?"

She turned to face him. "*Ya*."

Samuel glanced down at his feet, then looked out over the surrounding countryside. "Things are changing," he noted. *Whether I want them to or not.*

He finally returned his gaze to Hannah and offered her a small smile. It was tinged with more sadness than joy, but she didn't seem to realize it.

She wrapped her arms around him in a hug. "*Danki* for understanding my need to do this."

Samuel savored the opportunity to hold her close.

He didn't want to let her go.

Finally, he forced himself to release her. "Go and chase your dreams, Hannah." *I'll be waiting here for you when you come back*, he pledged silently.

❈ ❈ ❈

Ruth walked down the hallway to her bedroom, passing the open door of Hannah's room. She glanced inside, noticing her sister packing a suitcase.

Ruth stopped short, stepping through the doorway. "I can't believe you're really leaving. I'm going to miss you so much. But I'm proud of you for doing this."

"I'm proud of both of us for following our

dreams and not allowing others' opinions to stop us."

Ruth remained silent, not certain that she actually would be continuing with her art. She didn't want to risk bringing more trouble on her family because of her actions.

A figurative wide ugly gash ran right through the middle of their local Amish community, like a jagged ravine after an earthquake.

Was there any way to bridge the divide? Or was there an irreparable rift? No one seemed willing to stand in the shoes of the opposing stance to try to look at the situation from the other side and find middle ground.

With the two sides adamantly adhering to such different outlooks, how could they ever hope to reach a compromise that would satisfy everyone? It was a stalemate.

And now there was another threat on the horizon.

During her last visit to town, she heard that a group of *Englischers* had started buying up land on the edge of the town limit. Conservative members of the community were anti outsiders further encroaching on their traditional way of life, while the more progressive members were optimistic that this could bring new opportunities to the area.

Ruth wondered what new trials might be in store for her family and friends in the days ahead. She prayed that they would be able to find a way to repair the rift in their community and that both she and Hannah could somehow manage to bridge their traditions and their dreams.

❋ ❋ ❋

Did you enjoy your trip to Lancaster County? Find out more of what happens to Hannah and Ruth. The Lancaster Bridges series explores a close-knit Amish community in Pennsylvania as they navigate the challenges of a rapidly changing world. Experience the beauty and simplicity of Amish culture, while also witnessing the characters' journeys of self-discovery, personal growth, and community building. Overall, the series offers a rich and heartfelt portrayal of a community that is both deeply traditional and open to change, and celebrates the enduring values of family, faith, and love.

❋ ❋ ❋

The Bridge of Trust (Lancaster Bridges Book 1)
David Lantz has just returned from the *Englisch* world and becomes involved in efforts to rebuild the Fisher family's barn. As David and Ruth Fisher's relationship blossoms, tensions rise within the community over the direction of the Amish way of life. David must decide whether to accept an offer to work on a construction project in the outside world or stay and build a life with Ruth within the community. Will David and Ruth's love be enough to overcome the obstacles they face?

Meanwhile, Hannah Fisher struggles to reconcile her desire for change with her Amish beliefs, and tensions come to a head as different factions within the community clash over the direction of the Amish way of life. With the community divided between conservative and progressive factions, can they bridge the gap between tradition and modernity?

❊ ❊ ❊

The Bridge of Progress (Lancaster Bridges Book 2)
The Bridge of Solace (Lancaster Bridges Book 3)
The Bridge of Forgiveness (Lancaster Bridges Book 4)
The Bridge of Belonging (Lancaster Bridges Book 5)

Thank you, readers!

Thank you for reading this book. It is important to me to share my stories with you and that you enjoy them. May I ask a favor of you? If you enjoyed this book, would you please take a moment to leave a review on Amazon and/or Goodreads? Thank you for your support!

Also, each week, I send my readers updates about my life as well as information about my new releases, freebies, promos, and book recommendations. If you're interested in receiving my weekly newsletter, please go to newsletter.sylviaprice.com, and it will ask you for your email. As a thank-you, you will receive several FREE exclusive short stories that aren't available for purchase!

Blessings,
Sylvia

BOOKS BY THIS AUTHOR

Sarah (The Amish Of Morrissey County Prequel)

Available for FREE on Amazon
Welcome to Morrissey County! This fictional region in Pennsylvania Amish country is home to several generations of strong-willed Amish women who know what they want in life, even if others disagree. Join these women on their search for love and acceptance.

Morrissey County, 1979
Sarah Kauffman has always abided by the Ordnung, and not only because her father happens to be the town's bishop and would, she feels, disown her if she didn't. But when her mother passes away, she longs to escape the clutches of her father and run away to the Englisch world. When her father wants her to marry someone she doesn't love, Sarah becomes even more desperate to leave.

Jacob Renno, on the other hand, is happy with life on his farm. It keeps him so busy that the older bachelor has no time for love, but on lonely nights, he finds himself longing for a companion.

When Sarah and Jacob meet, there's an instant connection, but things get complicated. Jacob offers to help Sarah with her dilemma, but Bishop Kaufmann insists that she obey his wishes. Will Sarah run off to join the Englisch, or will the handsome farmer give her pause? Will her father disown her or give her his blessing? Find out in this sweet Amish romance as you become immersed in the lives of these Morrissey County residents.

Sarah is the prequel to the Amish of Morrissey County series. Each book is a stand-alone read, but to make the most of the series, you should consider reading them in order.

The Origins Of Cardinal Hill (The Amish Of Cardinal Hill Prequel)

Available for FREE on Amazon
Two girls with a legacy to carry on. A third choosing to forge her own path.
Welcome to Cardinal Hill, Indiana! This quaint fictional town is home to Faith Hochstetler, Leah Bontrager, Iris Mast, their families, and their trades. Faith, Leah, and Iris are united in their shared

passion for turning their hobbies within nature into profitable businesses…and finding love! Find out how it all begins in this short, free prequel!

Other books in this series:
The Beekeeper's Calendar: Faith's Story
The Soapmaker's Recipe: Leah's Story
The Herbalist's Remedy: Iris's Story

The Origins of Cardinal Hill is the prequel to the Amish of Cardinal Hill series. Each book is a stand-alone read, but to make the most of the series, you should consider reading them in order.

A Promised Tomorrow (The Yoder Family Saga Prequel)

Available for FREE on Amazon
The Yoder Family Saga follows widow Miriam Yoder and her four unmarried daughters, Megan, Rebecca, Josephine, and Lillian, as they discover God's plans for them and the hope He provides for a happy tomorrow.

The Yoder women struggle to survive after Jeremiah Yoder succumbs to a battle with cancer. The family risks losing their farm and their livelihood. They are desperate to find a way to keep going. Will Miriam and her daughters be able to work together to keep their family afloat? Will God pull through for them and provide for them in their time of need?

A Promised Tomorrow is the prequel to the Yoder Family Saga. Join the Yoder women through their journey of loss and hope for a better future. Each book is a stand-alone read, but to make the most of the series, you should consider reading them in order. Start reading this sweet Amish romance today that will take you on a rollercoaster of emotions as you're welcomed into the life of the Yoder family.

The Christmas Cards: An Amish Holiday Romance

Lucy Yoder is a young Amish widow who recently lost the love of her life, Albrecht. As Christmas approaches, she dreads what was once her favorite holiday, knowing that this Christmas was supposed to be the first one she and Albrecht shared together. Then, one December morning, Lucy discovers a Christmas card from an anonymous sender on her doorstep. Lucy receives more cards, all personal, all tender, all comforting. Who in the shadows is thinking of her at Christmas?

Andy Peachey was born with a rare genetic disorder. Coming to grips with his predicament makes him feel a profound connection to Lucy Yoder. Seeking meaning in life, he uses his talents to give Christmas cheer. Will Andy's efforts touch Lucy's heart and allow her to smile again? Or will Lucy, herself, get in his way?

The Christmas Cards is a story of loss and love and the ability to find yourself again in someone else. Instead of waiting for each part to be released, enjoy the entire Christmas Cards series in this exclusive collection!

The Christmas Arrival: An Amish Holiday Romance

Rachel Lapp is a young Amish woman who is the daughter of the community's bishop. She is in the midst of planning the annual Christmas Nativity play when newcomer Noah Miller arrives in town to spend Christmas with his cousins. Encouraged by her father to welcome the new arrival, Rachel asks Noah to be a part of the Nativity.

Despite Rachel's engagement to Samuel King, a local farmer, she finds herself irrevocably drawn to Noah and his carefree spirit. Reserved and slightly shy, Noah is hesitant to get involved in the play, but an unlikely friendship begins to develop between Rachel and Noah, bringing with it unexpected problems, including a seemingly harmless prank with life-threatening consequences that require a Christmas miracle.

Will Rachel honor her commitment to Samuel, or will Noah win her affections?

Join these characters on what is sure to be a heartwarming holiday adventure! Instead of waiting for each part to be released, enjoy the entire Christmas Arrival series at once!

Amish Love Through The Seasons (The Complete Series)

Featuring many of the beloved characters from Sylvia Price's bestseller, The Christmas Arrival, as well as a new cast of characters, Amish Love Through the Seasons centers around a group of teenagers as they find friendship, love, and hope in the midst of trials. ***This special boxed set includes the entire series, plus a bonus companion story, "Hope for Hannah's Love."***

Tragedy strikes a small Amish community outside of Erie, Pennsylvania when Isaiah Fisher, a widower and father of three, is involved in a serious accident. When his family is left scrambling to pick up the pieces, the community unites to help the single father, but the hospital bills keep piling up. How will the family manage?

Mary Lapp, a youth in the community, decides to take up Isaiah's cause. She enlists the help of other teenagers to plant a garden and sell the produce. While tending to the garden, new relationships develop, but old ones are torn apart. With tensions mounting, will the youth get past their disagreements in order to reconcile and produce fruit? Will they each find love? Join them on their adventure through the seasons!

Included in this set are all the popular titles:
Seeds of Spring Love
Sprouts of Summer Love
Fruits of Fall Love
Waiting for Winter Love
"Hope for Hannah's Love" (a bonus companion short story)

Jonah's Redemption (Book 1)

Available for FREE on Amazon
Jonah has lost his community, and he's struggling to get by in the English world. He yearns for his Amish roots, but his past mistakes keep him from returning home.

Mary Lou is recovering from a medical scare. Her journey has impressed upon her how precious life is, so she decides to go on rumspringa to see the world.

While in the city, Mary Lou meets Jonah. Unable to understand his foul attitude, especially towards her, she makes every effort to share her faith with him. As she helps him heal from his past, an attraction develops.

Will Jonah's heart soften towards Mary Lou? What will God do with these two broken people?

Elijah: An Amish Story Of Crime And Romance

He's Amish. She's not. Each is looking for a change. What happens when God brings them together?

Elijah Troyer is eighteen years old when he decides to go on a delayed Rumspringa, an Amish tradition when adolescents venture out into the world to decide whether they want to continue their life in the Amish culture or leave for the ways of the world. He has only been in the city for a month when his life suddenly takes a strange twist.

Eve Campbell is a young woman in trouble with crime lords, and they will do anything to stop her from talking. After a chance encounter, Elijah is drawn into Eve's world at the same time she is drawn into his heart. He is determined to help Eve escape from the grips of her past, but his Amish upbringing has not prepared him for the dangers he encounters as he tries to pull Eve from her chaotic world and into his peaceful one.

Will Elijah choose to return to the safety of his family, or will the ways of the world sink their hooks into him? Do Elijah and Eve have a chance at a future together? Find out in this action-packed standalone novel.

Finding Healing (Rainbow Haven Beach Prequel)

Available for FREE on Amazon
Discover the power of second chances in this heartwarming series about love, loss, and a fresh start from bestselling author Sylvia Price.

After the death of her husband, Beth Campbell decides it's time for a fresh start. When she returns to her hometown in Nova Scotia, she discovers a beautiful old abandoned home by the seaside and imagines it as the perfect spot for her to run a bed and breakfast and finally have the chance to write a novel. But when she discovers that the house belongs to Sean Pennington, a man with whom she has a painful history, she begins to doubt her dream.

With the encouragement of her friends and newfound faith, Beth takes a chance on the dilapidated home and hires Sean as a skilled carpenter to help her restore it. As they work together to bring the old house back to life, Beth and Sean's shared history resurfaces, forcing them to confront unresolved feelings and past mistakes. Will they be able to forgive each other and move on, or will their complicated history keep them apart?

Join Beth on her journey of self-discovery and

forgiveness. This inspirational series will touch your heart and remind you that it's never too late to start again. It is perfect for fans of uplifting women's fiction and readers who enjoy stories of finding hope and joy in unexpected places.

Songbird Cottage Beginnings (Pleasant Bay Prequel)

Available for FREE on Amazon
Set on Canada's picturesque Cape Breton Island, this book is perfect for those who enjoy new beginnings and countryside landscapes.

Sam MacAuley and his wife Annalize are total opposites. When Sam wants to leave city life in Halifax to get a plot of land on Cape Breton Island, where he grew up, his wife wants nothing to do with his plans and opts to move herself and their three boys back to her home country of South Africa.

As Sam settles into a new life on his own, his friend Lachlan encourages him to get back into the dating scene. Although he meets plenty of women, he longs to find the one with whom he wants to share the rest of his life. Will Sam ever meet "the one"?

Get to know Sam and discover the origins of the Songbird Cottage. This is the prequel to the rest of the Pleasant Bay series.

The Crystal Cresent Inn Boxed Set (Sambro Lighthouse Complete Series)

Amazon bestselling author Sylvia Price's Sambro Lighthouse Series, set on Canada's picturesque Crystal Crescent Beach, is a feel-good read perfect for fans of second chances with a bit of history and mystery all rolled into one. Enjoy all five sweet romance books in one collection for the first time!

Liz Beckett is grief-stricken when her beloved husband of thirty-five years dies after a long battle with cancer. Her daughter and best friend insist she needs a project to keep her occupied. Liz decides to share the beauty of Crystal Crescent Beach with those who visit the beautiful east coast of Nova Scotia and prepares to embark on the adventure of her life. She moves into the converted art studio at the bottom of her garden and turns the old family home into The Crystal Crescent Inn.

One of her first visitors is famous archeologist, Merc MacGill, and he's not there to admire the view. The handsome bachelor believes there's an undiscovered eighteenth-century farmstead hidden inside the creeks and coves of Crystal Crescent, and Liz wants to help him find it.

But it's not all smooth sailing at the inn that overlooks the historic Sambro Lighthouse. No one has realized it yet, but the lives of everyone in Liz's family are intertwined with those first settlers who landed in Nova Scotia over two hundred and fifty years ago. Will they be able to unravel the mystery? Will the lives of Liz's two children be changed forever if they discover the link between the lighthouse and their old home?

Take a trip to Crystal Crescent Beach and join Liz, her family, and guests as they navigate the storms and calm waters of life and love under the watchful eye of the lighthouse and its secret.

ABOUT THE AUTHOR

Now an Amazon bestselling author, Sylvia Price is an author of Amish and contemporary romance and women's fiction. She especially loves writing uplifting stories about second chances!

Sylvia was inspired to write about the Amish as a result of the enduring legacy of Mennonite missionaries in her life. While living with them for three weeks, they got her a library card and encouraged her to start reading to cope with the loss of television and radio, giving Sylvia a new-found appreciation for books.

Although raised in the cosmopolitan city of

Montréal, Sylvia spent her adolescent and young adult years in Nova Scotia, and the beautiful countryside landscapes and ocean views serve as the backdrop to her contemporary novels.

After meeting and falling in love with an American while living abroad, Sylvia now resides in the US. She spends her days writing, hoping to inspire the next generation to read more stories. When she's not writing, Sylvia stays busy making sure her three young children are alive and well-fed.

Subscribe to Sylvia's newsletter at newsletter.sylviaprice.com to stay in the loop about new releases, freebies, promos, and more. As a thank-you, you will receive several FREE exclusive short stories that aren't available for purchase!

Learn more about Sylvia at amazon.com/author/sylviaprice and goodreads.com/sylviapriceauthor.

Follow Sylvia on Facebook at facebook.com/sylviapriceauthor for updates.

Join Sylvia's Advanced Reader Copies (ARC) team at arcteam.sylviaprice.com to get her books for free before they are released in exchange for honest reviews.

Printed in Great Britain
by Amazon